For my children
with love and hope
D.G.

First published in Great Britain in 2008 by Bloomsbury Publishing Plc
36 Soho Square, London, W1D 3QY

Text & illustrations copyright © Debi Gliori 2008
The moral right of the author/illustrator has been asserted

A CIP catalogue record of this book is available from the British Library

ISBN 978 0 7475 9540 3

Printed in Belgium by Proost

1 3 5 7 9 10 8 6 4 2

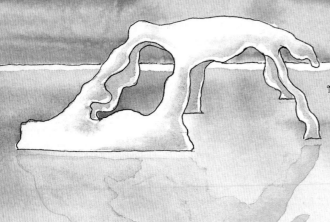

FSC
Mixed Sources
Product group from well-managed
forests and recycled wood or fibre
Cert no. BV-COC-070303
www.fsc.org
© 1996 Forest Stewardship Council

The papers on which this book is printed are manufactured from a composition of © 1996 Forest Stewardship Council A.C. (FSC) approved and post-consumer
waste recycled materials. The FSC promotes environmentally appropriate, socially beneficial and economically viable management of the world's forests

www.bloomsbury.com/childrens

The Trouble With Dragons

Debi Gliori

BLOOMSBURY
CHILDREN'S
BOOKS

The trouble with Dragons is . . .
Dragons make Dragons
and they make some more
till there are wall~to~wall Dragons
making Dragons galore.

Then Dragons start spreading all over the place . . .

soon their houses and roads take up all of the space.

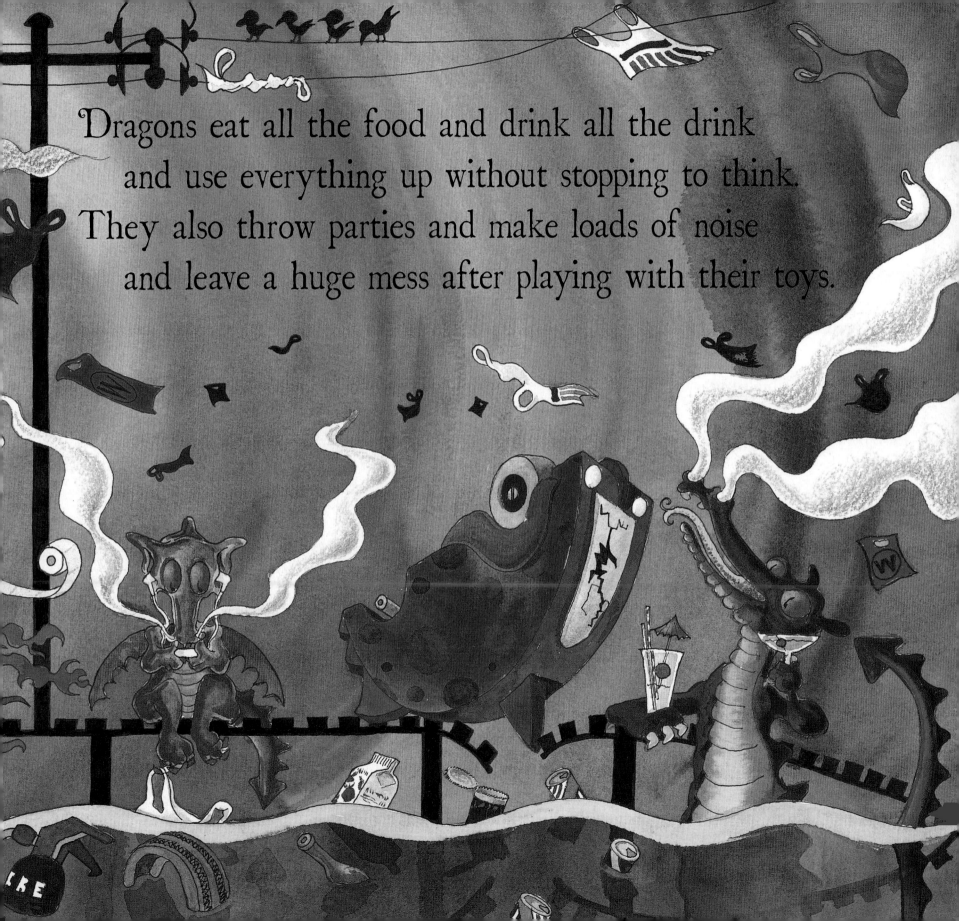

Dragons eat all the food and drink all the drink
and use everything up without stopping to think.
They also throw parties and make loads of noise
and leave a huge mess after playing with their toys.

Dragons chop down the forests,
which melts both the Poles,
and puncture the atmosphere
full of big holes.

Dragons blow out hot air,

which makes everything hotter...

and hotter...

and hotter...

until all the snow melts

and the ice turns to water.

Then the seas start to rise
and the deserts expand,
until everything's
covered
in water
or sand.

Say goodbye to the world
into which you were born.
Soon everyone else
will have packed up
and gone.

Everyone . . .
except the Dragons.
Poor Dragons.

Imagine a world with no birds and no bees,
just Dragons as far as a Dragon can see.
'Don't go,' wailed the Dragons.
'Don't leave us alone.
A world without wildlife
is no kind of home.'

'If you stay, we all promise
to do what it takes

to look after the planet
for all of our sakes.'

As the waters rose higher,
right over their knees,
a voice said,

'OK, start by **not** chopping down trees.'

Then all of the animals
chimed in with advice.

From the greatest of elephants

to the smallest of mice.

Eat food
that is grown
much closer to home.

And
leave
the wild places
and
ice caps

alone.

Stop blowing all that hot air
but instead choose to walk.

And put
less of our worl
on the end
of your
fork.

Respect all Earth's creatures
and cherish the land,
recycle, reuse and reduce
your demands.

So ~ if you know a Dragon
(and most of us do)
ask it if it thinks
that this story is true.

For if we can't see that
our stories are linked
then sadly,
like Dragons,
we'll soon be
extinct.